THE 4 CLANS OF SATON

ELIJAH SALMON

WORKBOOK PRESS LLC
187 E Warm Springs Rd,
Suite B285, Las Vegas, NV 89119, USA

Website: https://workbookpress.com/
Hotline: 1-888-818-4856
Email: admin@workbookpress.com

Ordering Information:
Quantity sales. Special discounts are available on quantity purchases by corporations, associations, and others. For details, contact the publisher at the address above.

ISBN-13:   978-1-953839-97-8 (Paperback Version)
                978-1-953839-97-8 (Digital Version)

REV. DATE: 04.02.2020

My name is Jesse Zeta of the Ookami Kyuketsuki clan also known as Kami Kyuketsuki. We are a heterogeneous of wolves and vampires. We are the original family of our masters Leon, Cleo, and Leona that made our clan. They were mercenaries of their clans that were sworn enemies. Master Leon was from the vampire clan, mistress Cleo was from the wolves' clan and her sister Leona was from the same clan. They had met when their two clans where in a truth period both clans had to do a co-op mission where they sent out their top candidates that would succeed their clans.

The wolves sent Mistress Cleo and mistress Leona while the vampires sent Master Leon. They were told to go and retrieve an item that had a sealed demon of sorts in it. After they were told what to do, they had gone to find this item but not knowing that their clan's leaders had other plans for them to be killed by the demon, so war would break out. Me and my family are direct descendants of their line. My father and mother are the leaders of our clan Ookami Kyuketsuki, one of the major clans.

There are four clans made of different heterogeneous groups. They have two leaders, an assistant, and a strategist of each clan. The leaders of our clan are Chris and Taylor, whom are my parents and clan leaders. We have a strategist whom you cannot know unless you are clan leaders. Being the leader of the clan, you have to be the reincarnation of our masters' Leon, Cleo, and Leona. But the reincarnation happens once every two generations.

If your generation is not the generation for the reincarnation of our masters, you have to go through trials and meet standards to become the leader. The trial and standards are different for the male and female. There are twelve candidates but the trials are life threatening.

They are choosing from the branch families of our clan being that my generation is the generation of the reincarnation we were raised with high expectations. But being that there is no way of knowing who the reincarnation of our masters are without the signs that start appearing on our 18th birthday for males and females. Those that have shown signs of us being the reincarnation, have to do the trial. The same as the clan leaders that were not the reincarnation of our masters.

Being that, I have shown signs of being the reincarnation of master Leon, we meet at my family dining hall. We, the candidates meet for our meeting and for our compatible test with chosen female heterogeneous who have shown signs of being a chance of being reincarnated as Cleo and Leona. The test to see if we are equal in power and spirit, to see if we are able to give birth to a strong child and to merge together to show we are the reincarnation of our masters.

We are not able to find out until we finish

our trials and drink the blood of our master Leon, mistress Cleo, and mistress Leona. If we are accepted by the blood, we will get the power and memories of Leon, Cleo, and Leona. After, we must battle each other to see who will be the head leader of the clan. Even though both will lead but two will be the head. The other assisted and strategist then they will be wed to Leon being that Cleo and Leona were also lovers as well as husband and wife. In the 4 clans you're allowed to have 2 wives and a mistress but Master Leon took both as his wife even though some wonder why. They say only the reincarnation knows why.

Sometimes there is love that's already between the vessels, that are the ones who have been chosen to be the reincarnation of master Leon, mistress Cleo and mistress Leona. We line up in the dining hall so the instructors can do the compatibility between the males and females, but we do not find out who our match is, until the trials are over.

As I reached the front of the line, I saw my two childhood friends who are from branch families. Rin Kappa, her family is skilled in assassination and information gathering. They are the most skilled out of all the families in the clan. Lynna Nu her family is also a branch family that is skilled in finding enemies bases and trackers. The Kappa's and Nu's may be branch families, but they also carry the bloodline of our masters Leon, Cleo and Leona but being that our family the Zeta, carries the strongest possibility of the bloodline of our masters and with our overwhelming power over them they became branch families.

So, they are also descendants of our masters so they do not become servants like the other branch families. They may have the blood lineage of master Leon, Cleo, and Leona but have not shown signs of compatibility of giving birth to vessels of master Leon, mistress Cleo and mistress Leona unlike Zeta, Kappa and Nu. That being said, the Nu family are descendants of our masters but have not shown any signs of having vessels for two reincarnation, the Kappa's haven't for three to four years of our masters until now.

Only my family, the head branch, has since the first leaders of our clan. Our masters formed our Maine and the three branches. Master Leon, Cleo and Leona had made the 3 clans Zeta, Kappa, Nu their kids become the leaders of the 3 clans. Zeta clan, the Maine family, Kappa, and Nu became the branch. Leon's son was the head of Zeta, the daughters of Cleo and Leon was the leader of Kappa and the daughter of Leona and Leon was the leader of Nu. The three of them had also wedded and had kids. The first son or daughter became the head of the three families if they had more kids, they would make the other branch families. The leader of the three families had to wed to make sure the line of succession would stay as pure blood as possible but being that, they couldn't tell which gender the baby would be sometimes outsiders would be brought in to give birth to the next head.

Luckily, that had only happened in the other families beside the Zeta's, Kappa's and Nu's. The instructor calls my name Jesse Zeta. Next, I say yes coming sir the instructor asks when I turned eighteen, I say march he says okay, touch the orb and transfer your energy into it. I ask if I need to transform, he says yes, I say okay when you transform you call out the meaning of your name. I call the meaning of my name wolves general. I changed into my heterogeneous form. In my form my hair grows longer and turns from silver to black, my eyes turn red, my ears grow longer and narrow with fur on them. My teeth change to fangs my hands turn into claws and my feet turn narrow and long. Then the energy of my powers combines after I'm done transforming. I touch the orb and transfer my energy of my power into it. When I do, the orb changes to red the instructor tells me to stop as I do.

I look at the instructor he says okay, but he seemed nervous and calls for the next person. As I'm changing back to my normal state my hair goes back silver my eyes go back to yellow and teeth go back to normal so does my hands a feet my energy goes back to being a vampire and my body goes back to being cold. The instructor tells me to go to the dining hall. I say okay and make my way there. When I'm leaving the dining room I see Rin and Lynna in their transformed state the girls are vampires in their transformed state they are wolves so their wolves Eniger appear more dominant just like when the guy transform to our vampire state. I hear Lynna call out to me and she's with Rin they run up me and hug me I say Rin, Lynna how have y'all been I haven't seen you too in 3 years. Rin says my parents had ordered her to start training to be a vessel for master Cleo. Lynna says her parents started training her the ways of her family became the most skilled trackers and finding enemies base when she was in training, she shown signs of becoming a vessel. As we were talking other people were walking pass us to go to the dining hall for our meeting I had said let's catch up. As we head to the meeting they said okay, I say that my parents have also been training me to become a vessel in the way of leading an army but they really were training me to become a warrior that can lead our people in war and as the leader of our clan.

As I'm talking to Rin and Lynna an instructor walks up to us asking are you 3 Jesse Zeta, Lynna Nu, and Rin Kappa we say yes. He says your family leaders want to talk to us together privately so go to the clan leader's bedroom. We say okay and I show Rin and Lynna to my parents' bedroom. As I am showing them to my parents' room our parents surprise us by coming to meet us on the way there. I say hi head leader an assistant leader mom says didn't I tell you when where not in formal meeting with everyone to call us mom and dad I say yes but you are with Rin and Lynna parents. Dad says it's fine when they're around only when in a meeting like in the dining room, I have to call them that. I say okay and greet Rin's and Lynn's parents by saying hi it's been too long since I last saw you. Rin and Lynna run to their parents and hug them they say let's go to the room. As we enter the room, they tell us to sit we say okay. My parents asked us what color the orb turned when we transferred our energy into it. I say mine turned red Rin says yellow and Lynna say hers turned silver. Our parents turn a look at each other and turn back to look at us and say what we are going to say must stay between us and no one else. We say okay my parents start out by saying you 3 know about our masters Leon, Leona, and Cleo right, we nod our heads they say good okay. Well, there's one more master that we have in the clan that has a reincarnation of her. Her name is master Lilla. She is also the wife of Leon's and sister to master Leon. But she was different then both of them she may have been heterogeneous, but she could turn to a weapon, but she would have to be wed to someone she would be bonded with. But the person also had to have partners that was in love with each other to and merge as one to wield her to her full potential.

Rin asks what does this have to do with us her parents says Rin the real reason we hold the compatibility test is to see who has the strongest compatibility of being the reincarnation of master Leon, master Cleo, master Leona, Lilla the trial had already started for us. The other 9 that had shown signs are not going to be taking the same trial as the 3 of you. They will be tested to see if they can wake the powers inside you 3 and once, they are tested you 3 will fight each other to awaken your powers. Then the 3 of you will fight to see who the 2 head leaders will be. After fighting the other 2 will be assistant, and strategist of the clan leader. I had asked why you are so sure that I'm master Leon reincarnation and that Rin and Lynna are master Cleo and masters Leona reincarnation. Mom says the compatibility test orb changes color to show who the vessel of our masters is.

The other way we confirm it is by the color of the orb that the vessel had. Then we have the vessel drink the blood of the master will reincarnate into them getting their memories and power and feelings but you also keep your memories but your souls will become one with the masters of who is reincarnated in you. You will still be known as you but have the presence of the master that has chosen you. Mom tells dad to get the blood of the 3 master Lynna mom says she will help dad says thanks and they get up and go to the closet and grabs 3 boxes Lynna's mom grabs one from dad and brings it to us dad puts them on the floor in front of him and Rin, Lynna mom has put the one she has in front of her. Mom say give the boxes that has the name of the master that will be reincarnate in them.

Dad gives me a Rin's ours, Lynna's mom gives her to Lynna. Mines says master Leon and Rin says master Leona on Lynna's is master Cleo then Lynna mom leaves. Mom says open them and take 2 sips of the blood once you do go lay on the bed all 3 of you and sleep it takes a day for the blood to be fully in your system we say okay.

Before you do, we have one more thing to tell you Lynna mom comes back mom says you 3 are brother and sisters. When I'm getting ready to open my box I stop and say how is that possible they have their own dad. Mom says we made that up to keep you safe from outsiders and others in the family and branch families that wish to do you harm. She says our 3 fathers are Chris and that Lynna's, and Rin's mom are her sister. mom says once you drink the blood you 3 will know everything. Lynna and Rin asks if they can talk to me alone mom says yes and the others give their permission of it being okay. When they have left the room, I ask them what is wrong. Lynna and Rin look at each other and blush. Rin says do you want me to tell him before we talk about what we heard and drink the blood of our masters Lynna nods in agreement. Rin says okay Jesse we have been hiding something from you because we didn't not know if either one of us or you would be the reincarnation of our masters. I ask what is it Rin, Rin says me and Lynna love you always have but we didn't know if you did we didn't want you to know because we didn't know which of us would be a vessel.

But know that we get to keep our own wills

and only have our memories and powers combine with our masters and that we are brother sister we wanted you to know and both give me a kiss incase things become more difficult can we tell you or be with you. Lynna says so know you now our true feelings and that the feelings we get from our masters will only increase their own feelings. I say okay I'm glad you girls told me but I don't know how I fell and will have to think on it and give them a hug. Rin says okay where done and the parents come in and closes the door and sit, we open the boxes that have the blood in them and take out the vials that have the blood in them. We take the top off and take 2 sips when we do we transform mom says that we are accepted as the vessel of our masters and are told to lay down together so the blood can fully get in our system so we can become the reincarnation of our masters. We go to lay down. I get in the middle Lynna is my right as Rin is on my left, they ask me if they can hold my hand, I say sure and close my eyes.

I started having memories of master Leon and he was with master Cleo and master Leona they were on a path talking about if all 3 of them where reincarnate in the same generation that means that there will be another war between the darkness and the 4 clans will need the power of their masters that have been reincarnated in their chosen vessel.

Master Leona says that won't happen because the 3 of us will end the power of darkness. Master

Cleo says you are right Leona but this will be the hardest battle we have faced being why we left our clans that could not work out their differences and we wedded to Leon so we could use our power together to end this. Master Leon say do you hear that Leon says come to me Cleo and Leona they run to him as they do, they are surrounded by the soldiers of the darkness. The soldiers of the darkness attacks them master Leon, Cleo and Leona transform and start fighting the darkness off but as they are fighting them off master Leon gets injured severely Cleo, and Leona calls out to him Leon are you okay where coming. Master Leon does not reply, they run to him ripping a hole though the enemy to get to master Leon when they reach him, he's on the ground. Master Cleo and master Leona cry out to him asking him to reply as they get though the last of the soldiers around him.

He has be sliced in his stomach coughing up blood as he on the ground master Cleo fall at his side and master Leona goes to other and try to help him up and say your wound should heal why is it not. Master Leon opens his eyes and says is that you Leona she smiles and reply yea as tears fall down her face and look at her sister and says look, he's alive she left her head up and say Leon , Leon are you okay she has tears going down on her cheeks to. He says I'm sorry to have worried you Leona says you should be you idiot. He says don't make laugh and my wound should healed and Leona looks and says it's not healing Leon what happened as she asked, he says I need both of you to kiss me know! They ask why master Leon says just do it Leona goes first and Cleo goes after her when they do master Cleo, Leon, and master Leona merged. They turn into legendary warrior of their 3 clans known as Leheato.

They asked Leon why they needed to take this form but then sense why he had them transform. The boss of the darkness had appeared, and he was covered in black and gold armor but he was a hybrid just like them they could tell his energies and it was as a bear and ratel. As master Leon was going to ask what he wanted master Leon falls to one knee Cleo and Leona had said your injury has not healed we should retreat the hybrid in the armor said you look injured you should retreat even though I won't let you an attacks. Leon dodges and say Cleo, Leona I'm glad we meet and formed our clan that we left to our kids an told them that one important rule. They say Leon why are you saying this that's when they understand saying you are not going to use that move are you we already are on our last one even if it could freeze him we don't know for how long. Leon says if we get the chance to reincarnate it will be fine, they both say you don't know if we will but let's do this.

That's when I woke up I was the first to wake as if there was something that I wasn't meant to see or now then I look at Lynna we were holding hands but she was still holding my hand but tighter then when I had closed my eyes. She had tears falling down her cheeks. She reminded me of Cleo. Then I turned to check on Rin. She reminded me of Leona she was holding my hand has if she didn't want to let go of it. Lynna started to wake I turned to her. She opens her eyes and I ask if she was okay, she jumped up and hugged me saying yes, I am Leon. I asked did you get your memories to Cleo but I like if you still called me Jesse and I still want to call you Lynna. She says yes, yes that's fine we hear Leona waking Cleo almost rolls over me to get to Leona as if something might happen to her. I say Cleo, Leona is okay as I help Cleo get up with my arm she's on. I look back over to Rin accidentally calling her Leona like I just did twice with Lynna. She wakes to hug me too. The same as Lynna did but grabbing Lynna at the same time saying I want you to keep calling me Rin. We hug her back saying it's okay with both of them crying. Rin calls me Leon by accident and says I mean Jesse let me check your stomach I say okay. I lay back down and they both rub and look at it as they look relieved.

They fall faced forward towards the bed and hugged me again saying we're glad you okay Jesse as if they had the same memory as me. They say yea it was the last thing we've seen before opening our eyes. You had fell to the ground and we were calling out to you and you didn't reply to us when we got to you, you were on the ground.

Sliced in the stomach unconscious bleeding

out Lynna had fell to her knee on the right side of you and I was on the left we both was crying you was coughing blood then you had opened your eyes. You said sorry for making us worry Lynna had looked at me and said look, look he's awake. Rin said you should be idiot as you said don't make me laugh you all of a sudden. you asked us to kiss. Kiss you as she said nervously. As we asked why but you said just do it. Lynna kissed you first then me so we could merge and transform that's when we had understood.

The leader had appeared and you fell on your knee when you was on your knee you told us you was happy to had met us and to see our kids become the leaders of the clan we made. That's when the boss attacked, I say that's when I woke. Rin says we were still asleep we had did the move to seal him after me and Lynna had cast a spell to help us reincarnate even though we didn't know if it would work 100% .Lynna says Rin you forgot to bring up what the boss leader looked like and why we had done our last move to seal him. Rin say oh right and says the boss was a bear and ratel tail like heterogeneous. He said you look injured you should retreat not like I would let you. Lynna says she got to the part where he attacks, and Rin says yea me to, but she looked kind of sad. Lynna says I love you so much I wouldn't know what to do if we lost you Rin says yea, I feel the same. I ask are you too saying that or is Leona and Cleo.

They say didn't we tell you before this

happened that we I interrupt by saying I know but I'm saying this as Leon I love you 2 to that's why I am asking. They smile saying Leon finally said he's loves us he never been able to say that until know. Our parents come in asking are you three up Leon, Cleo, and Leona. I ask mom to still call me what you have always called me I am your son.

The girls agreed with me our parents nod and smile to know where still their kids but that we also have reincarnated successfully. I say know we know why you did what you did and say we are glad that we love you and even though we are siblings it doesn't change much. Then we ask our parents as the clan leaders if they had our weapons as Leon, Cleo, and Leona they say yes and goes and get them. As their gone Rin asked as herself Jesse I know that you love me and Lynna looks shocked Jesse says how did you know that the one thing that our parent doesn't know is that our blood only help awaken us but part of is already in the vessel and that part is their quirks and tendencies when you hugged us after you said you didn't know how to answer is the way Leon shows us his feeling I said how did you know that. That when master Leon whispers to me saying of course she would know since Cleo has fully awoken and he laughs saying Lynna may have act shocked but they know us better than we think I smirk and say you knew that to right Lynna.

She looks away and whistle I say I just can't hide anything from you two and let Leon take over he says you're still the same Cleo you helped Rin by telling her that. Cleo appears saying I have no clue what you mean and Leona hug's him saying we will always be able to tell how you fell. That when they come back with our weapons an say I see you helped our kids sort out how they fell Leon says it's no problem we favor them just as when you 3 where growing up.

They smile and hand them their weapons Leona asks if he has awakened, they say no but the spell has weakened and someone's is making it weak. Cleo says we understand I ask Leon if he sure don't he want to spend more time awake to spend with them Leona says it's okay we can later I'm sure you, Rin and Lynna have a lot to talk about, Cleo says we have a lot of time so enjoy yourself and the 3 of you can also communicate the same as we are and me, Rin, Lynna take over. I ask how did the trials go they say the candidates to awaken your powers and to get the chance to fight for head assistant, strategist clan leader have also been readied for you 3. I say 3 but there's 2 leaders, assistant, and a strategist in each family but then they call in there strategist saying there actually 4 and said we have 4 leaders is that technically it would be the strategist we keep them our strategist a secret to help plan our war efforts in our family.

We just make the rules and plan on how we live. The assistant help with our living father introduces their strategist her name is Hailey she is your sister jessie also the clan's strategist. I say wait I thought Rin and Lynna was my sibling oh wait you kept her a from just you did with Rin and Lynna. Mom says we couldn't tell you all this Jesse until you became Leon vessel. She is your 3rd sister and she has the soul of Lilla he seal that from the vessel to keep her safe an her powers have been sealed to Jesse she is a year younger than the 3 of you but also has the same power of Leona but not the same caliber.

Mom tell Hailey to kiss me, Rin and Lynna but me on the lips and to kiss them on the checks and everyone power limiter will be removed and seal will be removed so it can be awaken when the do the trial. She says mom but they are my siblings and that we had not wedded yet. Mom says with the power you hold you do not to an with the power you have you can forge one through you kiss with all 3 of them she I understand she kisses me on the lips and the other 2 on the check a power an memories flow though us as if a flood gate has opened up. Haley come back in front an smile saying brother do you remember me as your younger sis and as Leon that's when they finally stop I grab Hailey and say Haley is this really you she cries saying, yes I missed you so much and hugs me and kiss me again on the lips standing on her tip toes she put her head on my shoulder still hugging me I say I happy your her. The girls come running and hug her as well and say I'm so glad your safe.

I asked, does Maria want to see Leon, Leona, and Cleo being it been she says yes and we let go of each other and let our masters out. Leon says I'm just glad you're alive my little sister. I'm so glad your alive mom dad would be to if they knew this and that you can reincarnated even if we're not together ever reincarnation. Leon hugs her and let me take over again I let go of my sister and say we are complete now as Cleo and Leona hugs Hailey and say there glad we're together at last before the go back to Rin and Lynna. I ask mom and dad so do we fight soon they yes in 1hr I say okay let the 4 of sit here and get our plan together they say okay and leave.

Hailey says if we are really together, were really here am I not just dreaming? I say yes we're all together an I'm sorry for not calling you by your really I know you would like me to call you Lillia like I used to, but we all decide to go the name we have known Cleo and Leona agreed. Leona says I'm Lynna in this life , Cleo says she is Rin in this time, and I say I'm Jesse and that you can call us by our real names but we want to be called our name of this time. Hailey says okay big brother as she's holding my arm and I say so what's the plan for the 3 candidates. Rin says we should probably let you handle the main combated and Leona heals you and Rin will provide the regard support I say wait if it's supposed to be a 3on3 why do we have Hailey here mom says that she will not be fight just coming up with plan's like she did I say ahh okay I ask that where not supposed to use our supposed to use or once the other 3 bring them out if they can.

Dad says you are correct once it is brought your area will change once it does you will need to other retreat an hid until it get use to your vessel but if you force to fight try to only use you weapon nothing else otherwise you will awaken the master soul because their power only activate when you don't use you chosen weapons they can awaken without them but you will need them to which you will not be able to do in combat. Halie says isn't just as it is known when we switch in between know.

Master Leon takes over an says no the reason your able to know is because we are doing our self and we are let you keep control you will be able to fully call us forth when you understand us an your powers and not just enjoy them. I say master why don't you tell how to get control, he says Jesse you are one of the few that know too they can come together and treat them as separate being you can be told to do this you have to be will and accepting of us of your own free will. Halie say master what's wrong why have you gone quite he says sorry about that Jesse was talking to me about something. Leona says master Leon how is he able to do that when we can't master Leon says he says Jesse was able to meet a shorten requirement to be able it is different than the 4 of talk to each other. I say mast let me talk over before they catch on, they know us to well and they will try to get it out of us. He says okay I says sorry guys I accident let master out they oh okay and finish what he meant.

You have to not just be able to recall their previous lives you must be able to tell who they are an what they can do in order to do it. Without support a mind can become weak but with the support of other it will grow as an adult. The other 2 Lilla says Hailey says what that means but Rin sits there quietly as if she doesn't understand but gives a smile. I look and say hey Rin when was the first time we met and how did I get hurt. She says why are you asking me this? I reply by saying can you please answer she says you know it's not her don't you Jesse I say you have been reached this haven't you and Cleo says you noticed she reached the requirement level, didn't you. She says Rin and she comes out and says that's Jesse for you. How did you know and when did you notice?

I say do you think that I can't tell your souls apart? She says Jesse you shouldn't be able to do that, yet you haven't awoken. I say Rin stop the act you tell everyone what level aura you are at because you are stronger than all of us. Lilla says what are you guys talking I say Rin if you don't tell them I will. Because mom and dad don't even know how strong you are. Dad says what I say dad, mom, and sister Rin and Cleo are at high ascendant of the gods level aura and I'm only at high angel she is a level above me. Hailey you are the level of royal fairy and Leona and Lynna you are at the level of a warlord. I say that Rin and Cleo are on immortals of the gods aura level but being that she that she didn't ascend yet she still classified as high ascendant of the gods but she won't be after the trial and I won't neither but you two will unless you guys can reach the requirement that you need. I say mom dad out of all us Rin has always been able to be the strongest out of all of us but her vessel after the master died were not able to bring out even half of Rin power that's why master Leon has been the strongest but still even then none of our powers where close to half until today with me and Rin. Mom says we'll talk more about this another time but for now we need you guys to be ready for your trial after you finish your trials we will continue this conversation but get some rest for a couple hours and we will wake you when it is time. All 4 four of get into the bed and go to sleep when we do have a dream, well more of a memory of continuing when Leon was merged with Cleo and Leona fighting the demon. It was the part where they made sure we could reincarnate when I realized what they had done. I had woken up to them already woken up looking at me with an expression on their face saying I wasn't meant to remember that. They had started crying say Leon, Jesse we are so so sorry I look at them saying you guys have been manipulating me and my memory just so I wouldn't remember that and that this isn't first time I been reincarnated in Jesse you guys made this way same with your and that Rin, Lynna and Lilla know this but kept in the dark. I get up to leave the bed. They all grab me to prevent me from getting up. Rin switches with Cleo and says let me talk to Jesse. Leon says he doesn't want to talk you do you know how upset he is and how pissed I am at them but I mainly hurt for Jesse. Rin says please let me talk to him. Leon gets a message from Jesse and Leon says for him, he says if you leave him alone, he won't want anything to do with you. Rin lets go saying noo... no way he said that with an despair appearing one. Lynna come out and says Jesse Jesse please let us explain an then Leona come saying Leon please please we just didn't that's when I come saying Leave us alone and I have my aura burst out making them let go and say if you guys still want us to be able to forgive you leave us alone you got it. Rin looks up and try to say something but I shoot a look at her stopping her from saying whatever she was going to say and get up and out of the bed and start walking toward the door. That's when Lilla comes out saying big brother I just keep walking and she shout out big brother just like the day we both lost her that when image appear of when we lost her she was trying to save me and got stab in my place shouting my name. I stop and me and Leon speaking saying that not right Lilla, Hailey. They speak as one saying how else would I be able to make you stop I know no matter how mad you are or upset if you hear me call out like that you will stop and listen to what I have to say. You love me too much to not. We say you right but not this time being that you were apart of it and start walking and says our name in the same way Jesse, Leon. We start to cry and say Hailey, Lilla and say same way why why did you do that why how could you...you of out of them you as tears come out. They go quiet and we run towards the door bumping in to our parents and just keep going. I don't look at them because they were in on it too and they look toward Hailey saying he found out didn't he none of them reply. Mom says let's hope this the bond you 4 have will be able to handle this but you 3 know you will have to do the trials with just you 3 cause he will not do it with you right. He'll most likely solo it until when ya have to fight the other candidates. Leona comes out saying we know but we will not lose them because this we been through to make sure we could stay with Jesse and Leon they are the only for us me, Rin, Cleo, Hailey and Lilla will not accept anyone but them and no one else. Cleo says it took 300 hundred years to find vessels that felt the same way as us and wanted the same as so this could happen. To make sure we could always been in the same generating and keep our memories not just part we need our chosen vessel to feel the same way as we did before we became one and thanks to that these last 3 vessel we were able to stay together and keep that from him having him remember everything but that. Rin comes out saying right we are not losing Jesse not what we have to do to get him to forgive us we make sure we get him to. Lilla says right we have to or we will lose all of our memories of each other. The only thing we will know is that we started a clan together but not anything else..